DATE DUE

NOV 04

JAN 04 '06

JUN 28 NVC

00-07 NVC
JAN 28 '06

MAR 24 07

MAR 24 07

The Case Of The
Sundae Surprise

Look for more great books in

series:

The Case Of The Great Elephant Escape
The Case Of The Summer Camp Caper
The Case Of The Surfing Secret
The Case Of The Green Ghost
The Case Of The Big Scare Mountain Mystery
The Case Of The Slam Dunk Mystery
The Case Of The Rock Star's Secret
The Case Of The Cheerleading Camp Mystery
The Case Of The Flying Phantom
The Case Of The Creepy Castle
The Case Of The Golden Slipper
The Case Of The Flapper 'Napper
The Case Of The High Seas Secret
The Case Of The Logical I Ranch
The Case Of The Dog Camp Mystery
The Case Of The Screaming Scarecrow
The Case Of The Jingle Bell Jinx
The Case Of The Game Show Mystery
The Case Of The Mall Mystery
The Case Of The Weird Science Mystery
The Case Of Camp Crooked Lake
The Case Of The Giggling Ghost
The Case Of The Candy Cane Clue
The Case Of The Hollywood Who-Done-It

and coming soon

The Case Of Clue's Circus Caper

The Case Of The
Sundae Surprise

by Melinda Metz

■HarperEntertainment
An Imprint of HarperCollinsPublishers

PARACHUTE PRESS

Parachute Publishing, L.L.C.
156 Fifth Avenue
New York, NY 10010

DUALSTAR PUBLICATIONS

Dualstar Publications
c/o Thorne and Company
A Professional Law Corporati
1801 Century Park East
Los Angeles, CA 90067

HarperEntertainment

An Imprint of HarperCollins*Publishers*
10 East 53rd Street, New York, NY 10022

10 9 8 7 6 5 4 3 2 1

WE ALL SCREAM
FOR ICE CREAM

"Let's get started." Helen Sweeney clapped her hands. "Today is a very exciting day! Today I will have all your amazing new ice cream flavors in my ice cream shop for the grand opening!"

My twin sister, Ashley, took a big silver mixing bowl from the cabinet over our cooking station. She put it on the counter. "Okay, Mary-Kate," she said. "First we need milk."

Ashley is very organized. It's one of the

things that makes her a great detective. But today we weren't Olsen and Olsen, detectives. Today we were Olsen and Olsen, ice cream makers.

A group of our friends were ice cream makers today too. Tim Park and Patty O'Leary and Samantha Kramer were all entering the ice cream–making contest at Sweet Sundaes Ice Cream Shop with us.

We would all get a chance to invent a brand-new ice cream flavor. Over the next two days, Helen's customers would vote for the one that tasted the best. And whoever got the most votes for their ice cream would win a free sundae every week for a whole year!

"It's so cool how we each have our own little kitchen," Samantha called from her cooking station.

Helen smiled. Her blue eyes twinkled. "I'm glad you like them. I thought it would be fun for people to walk by Sweet

Sundaes and see their ice cream being made. I—"

"Aunt Helen," a girl named Melanie interrupted. "Can I have another apron? This one has a wrinkle." She pushed her curly red bangs out of her face.

"But it will still keep your clothes clean," Helen told her niece. "And that is what's important."

Melanie frowned. "Who wants to trade aprons with me? I'll give whoever trades a purple elephant sticker."

"I'll trade!" Samantha said.

I grinned. That was the third trade Melanie made today. She wants everything she has to be the best.

I grabbed a measuring cup and took the milk out of the mini-freezer at our cooking station. "How much do we need?" I asked Ashley.

Before she could answer, a boy with a

buzz cut burst into the store. "Am I too late to be in the contest?" he cried.

"Of course not," Helen said. "You can have that cooking station." She pointed to the one next to me and Ashley. "Tell us your name. Then I'll give you a quick lesson on ice cream making."

"Don't worry about that," the boy answered. "I know how to make ice cream already. I'm a sun-gei." He pretended to sweep a sword through the air. "That's 'genius' when you put the letters in a different order. It sounds like the name of a Jedi knight, right?"

Ashley and I looked at each other and giggled.

"You forgot to say your name, genius," Patty said.

"Charlie," the boy said. "Charlie Elliot, that's me."

"Good to meet you, Charlie," Helen said.

"My name is Helen Sweeney. You may call me Helen."

She turned to us. "The rest of you get started while I get Charlie set up."

"I'm going to get started with this," Tim announced. He grabbed a jar of bright red sauce and poured some right into his mouth. Then he popped in a few chocolate hearts and a handful of nuts.

"Don't eat all the ingredients before we get to them," I said.

"He's in hog heaven with all this food around," Ashley said.

I laughed. Eating is Tim's favorite hobby.

"Okay, Mary-Kate. We're ready to make our super-special ice cream flavor." Ashley mixed the milk and sugar together.

I put a layer of rock salt into the ice cream maker. Helen explained to us that the salt helps the milk get cold enough to turn into ice cream. Then Ashley mixed in some chocolate chunks. They looked good!

"Hey, who took my strawberries?" Patty called out.

"Not me," Tim mumbled through a mouthful of marshmallows.

"Strawberries…" Charlie scrunched up his face. Then he said, "Eat raw rats!"

I gulped. "Gross! What are you talking about, Charlie?"

Charlie grinned. "'Eat,' 'raw,' 'rats'—all those words are in the word 'strawberries.' I like it when I can make words out of other words. I do it all the time."

Ashley put our ice cream mix into the ice cream maker. I started to crank the handle. After I cranked long enough, we would have ice cream!

"Here you go." Melanie handed Patty a cup of strawberries and a cute little blue bobby pin. "I traded with you. Your berries were redder."

"You're supposed to ask before you trade," Patty told her.

"I didn't think you would mind," Melanie said.

I kept turning the crank on the ice cream maker. It got tougher to turn as the ice cream got colder and harder. "I think it's almost ready," I told Ashley.

"Then it's time for our super-secret special ingredient, Mary-Kate," Ashley whispered.

"Secret?" Charlie leaned over from his cooking station. "'See,' 'tree,' 'rest,' 'set.'"

"You have good hearing," I said. "Don't look, Charlie. It's a secret!" I turned to Ashley. "Don't say the name of our ingredient or somebody might hear. Just pour it in."

Ashley took a plastic bag out of her backpack. On the front of the bag were the words "The World's Best Gummy Oranges."

"You brought in your own ingredient?" Patty asked. "I didn't know we could do that."

I smiled. "It's something our great-grandma Olive sent us. You can't even buy our secret ingredient here in town."

"Hey, if anybody needs help coming up with the name for their ice cream, ask me," Charlie called. "I love word games—and I'm really good at scrambling letters."

Helen clapped her hands. "Okay, everyone. Your ice cream should be really hard to crank at this point. And that means it's done!"

"Yippee!" Tim cried. "Now comes my favorite part: the eating!"

"Almost," Helen said. "First you need to put your ice cream into one of the cardboard containers." She pointed to a row of brightly colored containers on the shelf under the window. "Then give me your recipe cards."

"We call orange!" Ashley exclaimed.

"Perfect," I agreed. "An orange container for orange ice cream."

Ashley got the bright orange container

and we filled it to the top with our brand-new flavor.

"Now it's time for tasting!" Tim announced. He waved a handful of plastic spoons.

"Try mine first," Samantha begged.

Ashley and I rushed over to her cooking station along with everyone else. Tim handed out the spoons.

"Yummy," Ashley said.

"Vanilla with cinnamon and a little bit of..." Charlie closed his eyes while he thought. "A little bit of maple syrup."

"You're exactly right," Samantha said. "I wanted my ice cream to taste like the French toast my mom makes."

"French toast? 'Soft,' 'star,' 'rotten,' 'neat,' 'honest,' 'not,' 'rat,' 'fat'..." Charlie's face lit up. "I know. How about 'for cats then'? That's the best. It uses up all the letters!"

Samantha wrinkled her nose. "I think I'll call it Mom's French Toast."

We went around the room, tasting and tasting and tasting.

I didn't know what to say about Charlie's flavor. It was…strange. He had put in so many ingredients, there was hardly any ice cream in his ice cream.

"I think the best one is—" Patty began.

"You haven't tasted mine yet!" Melanie interrupted. "It's called The Best of the Best. I used only the very best ingredients in the kitchen. So that means my ice cream will be the best."

We all dug our spoons into Melanie's container. Then the room was filled with "yums" and "mmm-mmms."

"This is the most fantastic ice cream I've ever tasted," Tim said. "It's even better than mine!"

Melanie grinned. "The best ingredients mean the best ice cream. I told you," she bragged.

"But you have one more flavor to try," Ashley said.

"That's right!" I said. I grabbed our bright orange bucket. "Get ready to experience Creamy Orange Choco Chunk."

Tim's spoon was the first one in. A second later his spoon was in again. "I could eat this all day!"

"I like it even more than my French toast flavor," Samantha said.

"I didn't know we could bring our own ingredients," Patty complained. "Now you guys are going to win."

"Time to get those containers in the big freezer," Helen told us. "But first I need someone to clear off a shelf."

"Mary-Kate and I will do it," Ashley said. We hurried to the big freezer in the kitchen and turned on the light. The small room was filled with shelves, like a closet. But the air was sooo cold!

"It's freezing in here," Ashley said. She handed me a carton of ice cream to put on another shelf.

"That's why they call it a freezer," I teased. "Work faster or we'll turn into ice sculptures before we're through."

Ashley handed me ice cream containers at triple speed. I moved them to different shelves just as fast.

"Done!" I cried.

"Let's get back where it's warm," Ashley said. She leaned on the freezer's big metal door.

It didn't open.

"Let me try." I pushed the door as hard as I could.

It didn't open.

Then Ashley and I pushed on the door together. It still didn't budge.

"It's locked!" Ashley exclaimed.

"We're trapped!" I cried.

2

Frozen!

"**W**e're going to freeze!" Ashley cried.

I pounded on the freezer door with both hands. *Bam! Bam!*

"Help!" Ashley screamed. She pounded on the door too.

I put my ear to the door. I couldn't hear anything. "Keep yelling," I said. "Maybe someone will hear us."

We both pounded on the door. I shivered. It was getting really cold! We kept pounding and yelling, yelling and pounding.

Finally, the door swung open. A blast of warm air hit my face. *Yes!*

"Helen, you saved us!" Ashley said.

Helen opened the freezer door wider. "Oh, my goodness! Hurry out and warm up."

We were out of the freezer before the words were out of her mouth. Helen grabbed our hands. "You're so cold! Let me make some hot chocolate for you."

"That's okay," I said. "We're fine. Really."

"Are you sure?" Helen's forehead was creased with worry. "I don't understand how this could have happened. The freezer door is specially designed so it won't lock automatically."

I looked at Ashley. She looked at me. I knew we were thinking the same thing. Did someone lock us in the freezer on purpose? We looked around. All the cooking stations were empty. Everyone had gone home.

Only Helen and Samantha were still here.

"I'm so sorry we didn't hear you right away," Helen continued. "Samantha and I were in my office. She was helping me make flyers announcing the contest."

"That's okay," I said again. "We weren't stuck for that long."

"Samantha, why don't you start moving the ice cream containers from the little freezers at the cooking stations to the big freezer?" Helen said. "I'll prop the door open with something just to be on the safe side."

Helen slid a chair against the open freezer door so it wouldn't close. Then she turned to me and Ashley. "Come into my office. I want to give you the flyers announcing the contest. You can hand them out to your friends."

We followed Helen to her little office. It was so cute. There was a mobile made of ice cream scoops hanging over her desk.

"Here you go." She gave me and Ashley a pile of flyers.

"I love the color," I said. The flyers were bright orange. Just like the container Ashley and I chose for our ice cream.

"Thanks," Helen answered. "Remember— the voting starts tomorrow."

"But what if you run out of our flavor?" I asked. "People won't be able to vote for it if there's none left."

"That's why I collected recipes from all of you," Helen told us. "I'll use the recipe to make more of a flavor if I need to."

"We can't wait to see which flavor wins," Ashley said. We headed back into the kitchen and over to our cooking station.

"It feels good to be warm again!" I said.

"Yeah!" Ashley agreed. She picked up her backpack. Then she frowned. "The floor is all sticky."

I glanced down. A trail of orange droplets covered the floor by our station.

"Uh-oh. That looks like our Creamy Orange Choco Chunk!" I exclaimed. "What if it melted before Samantha got it into the big freezer?"

We bolted over to the freezer. Samantha was about to shut the door.

"I can't believe you two want to go back in there," she said when she saw us.

"We just want to make sure our ice cream is okay," Ashley told her. We hurried into the freezer.

I could see my breath coming out of my mouth. That's how cold it was. What I couldn't see was our orange ice cream container.

"I guess you didn't move ours yet," Ashley said.

"Yes, I did. I just finished bringing in the last container," Samantha answered. She pointed to a light green container. "That's yours right there."

The container had our names on it. But it wasn't ours. Our container was bright orange.

Ashley grabbed the light green container and pulled off the lid. She turned the container toward me so I could see inside.

Plain vanilla!

"Someone stole our ice cream!" I cried.

THE THIEF STRIKES AGAIN!

Ashley turned to Samantha. "Are you sure this green container is the one you found in our mini-freezer?"

"I'm positive," Samantha said.

"What are we going to do?" I asked.

"We're detectives," Ashley answered. "We're going to find the thief. Come on, Mary-Kate."

"Do you think Samantha got our container mixed up with someone else's?" I whispered.

"I don't know," Ashley said. "But something strange is going on. Look!" She pointed to a trail of ice cream drops leading from our cooking station to the door.

I gasped. "The thief must have taken our ice cream while we were trapped in the freezer."

"I bet the thief is the one who locked us in the freezer in the first place!" Ashley exclaimed. "Helen said the door doesn't lock by itself."

"Okay, let's follow the orange-drop trail."

We followed the ice cream trail drop by drop. It led right to the back door. We went outside.

"There's another drop!" Ashley cried. She pointed to an orange drop glistening in the sun.

We followed the drops all the way across the parking lot. Then we followed them to the sidewalk.

Ashley stopped at the bus stop. "Mary-Kate! Look! I found our ice cream!"

Someone had thrown our ice cream container into the bushes. The bright orange color made it impossible to miss. I reached into the bushes and grabbed it.

Ashley yanked it open.

Our ice cream had totally melted into orange goop! The World's Best Gummy Oranges floated on top. All the chocolate chunks had sunk to the bottom.

"It's ruined," I moaned.

"It looks like someone wanted us out of the contest," Ashley said. "And we're going to find out who it is. Let's go back to Sweet Sundaes. Maybe our thief left some more clues behind."

"Right," I said. "I hope Samantha is still there. We have to ask her some more questions."

We ran back to the ice cream shop.

Helen rushed over to us. "Samantha told me what happened," she exclaimed. "I'm so sorry. I can't believe someone took your ice cream!"

"Samantha, was anyone else around when you moved the cartons into the freezer?" I asked. "Did anyone come back because they forgot something?"

"No. I was all by myself," Samantha answered. A horn honked outside. "My mom's waiting. See you tomorrow!"

"Oh, dear," Helen said. "I wish I had moved the containers. Then I would have known something was wrong. All my containers are bright colors. I don't have any pale green ones."

Ashley pulled out her detective notebook and wrote down the fact that Helen didn't have pale green ice cream containers. That could be an important clue.

Helen picked up two aprons from the

counter and handed them to me and Ashley. "I think you two have another batch of ice cream to make."

"Really?" Ashley said. "You'll let us make it over?"

"Of course," Helen said. "I can't open my ice cream store tomorrow without Creamy Orange Choco Chunk!"

"I'll get the milk!" Ashley cried. "I remember that ingredient!"

"I'll go get your recipe card," Helen said.

"And I'll get our secret ingredient." I unzipped Ashley's backpack and opened the bag of gummy oranges.

"Oh, no!" I said. "You are not going to believe this!"

"What's wrong?" Ashley asked.

"Our super-special super-secret ingredient is gone!"

4

NOT TIM!

I handed Ashley the bag that had held our gummy oranges.

Ashley peered inside. "Polka-dot jelly beans!" she said. "Someone stole our gummy oranges and replaced them with jelly beans! What are we going to do? We can't make our special flavor without our secret ingredient."

I snapped my fingers. "I know! We'll call Great-grandma Olive and ask her to send us more gummy oranges by overnight mail."

"Yes! We can have them by tomorrow morning," Ashley said. "We'll mix up a new batch of ice cream now. We'll come over here first thing in the morning and add them!"

We still had a chance to win the contest. I could almost taste those free ice cream sundaes. A whole year's worth!

Helen walked back into the kitchen. "We need to come in tomorrow morning before you open and add just one thing to our new batch of ice cream. Is that okay?" I asked.

Helen didn't answer. She just shook her head. "I'm so sorry, girls," she said. "I found the envelope that held your recipe card. But now the envelope is empty!"

"The thief thought of everything!" Ashley exclaimed. "He or she even took our recipe. Now we can't make more of our flavor."

"At least we didn't say what our secret

ingredient was in the recipe," I reminded Ashley. "We just wrote down 'one cup of the secret ingredient.'"

"But Mary-Kate, the thief stole the secret ingredient too!" Ashley answered.

"Do you think the two of you can remember your recipe?" Helen asked.

"I don't think I can," I admitted. I turned to Ashley.

"Me neither," she said. "We tried a bunch of things before we came up with our flavor."

"How about creating a brand-new flavor?" Helen suggested.

"But Creamy Orange Choco Chunk was so yummy," Ashley said.

I sighed. "Everyone loved it," I said. "Especially Tim!"

Ashley turned to Helen. "Do you think you could start the contest on Sunday instead of tomorrow?" she asked. "I know

Mary-Kate and I can solve the case and get back our recipe before Sunday."

"Yes!" Helen exclaimed. "That's a perfect idea. We'll call it the Super Sunday Sundae Contest."

"We'll need to start searching for clues in the kitchen," I said. "Is that okay?" I asked Helen.

"Of course," she said. "I'll be in the office if you need me." She headed for the door.

"Let's go over this again," Ashley said. "The last time we saw our ice cream was before we went into the freezer, right?"

"Right," I answered. "The thief must have switched ice cream cartons when we were inside."

"And we were in there for about ten minutes," Ashley said. "That would be enough time for the thief to make the switch, grab the gummy oranges, and take our recipe."

I walked over to the freezer and studied the door. I touched the handle. It was sticky, and my fingers were stained red. I took a taste. Cherry sauce! "The thief had cherry sauce on his or her fingers," I announced.

I opened my backpack and pulled out the bag our gummy oranges had been in. There was cherry sauce on it too! I showed the bag to Ashley.

"Good job, Mary-Kate." Ashley wrote down our new clue in her detective note-book. She wrote "polka-dot jelly beans" as a clue too.

"We need to figure out who touched the cherry sauce today. Anyone who touched it has to go on our list of suspects," Ashley said.

"That's horrible!" I said.

"Why?" Ashley asked. Her forehead got all wrinkly. She always wrinkles her forehead when she doesn't understand something.

"Don't you remember? Tim ate some cherry sauce straight out of the jar!" I told her.

Ashley frowned. Then she flipped open her detective notebook. "I don't want to do this," she said. "But I have to."

She wrote the word "suspects" in her notebook. Then under that she wrote "Tim."

5

SUSPECTS,
SUSPECTS, SUSPECTS

"**A**shley, do you really think Tim stole our ice cream?" I asked.

"I don't know," Ashley said. "Let's not jump to conclusions. Other people might have used the cherry sauce today."

"Right." I let out a long breath. Tim was our best friend. I really, really didn't want him to be our thief.

"Let's ask Helen if anyone used cherry sauce in his or her recipe," I suggested.

"Great idea!" Ashley grabbed my hand. We flew out of the kitchen and into Helen's office. She was working at her desk.

"Helen, we need to know if anyone used cherry sauce in his or her recipe," I said.

Helen picked a stack of envelopes off her desk. "I can't show you the recipes," she answered. "After all, it's still a contest! But I'll look at them and tell you who used cherry sauce."

She began to open the envelopes. "This is the one your recipe should have been in. It's the only empty one." Helen handed the envelope to Ashley.

Ashley held it up so I could see the red stain on the flap.

"Cherry sauce," I said.

Helen began reading the recipes. "No cherry, no cherry, no cherry," she muttered as she flipped through the recipes. She sat up straighter. "Cherry!"

"Whose recipe is that?" I demanded.

"Charlie's," Helen answered.

"Of course. Charlie put everything on the table in his ice cream," Ashley said. "There wasn't room for any ice cream when he was done."

Helen read some more. "No cherry, no cherry, no cherry, no cherry." There was only one envelope to go. Helen opened it. "Cherry!"

"Great!" Ashley said. "Whose is it?"

"My niece Melanie's," Helen said. She looked up at us. "Oh, dear. I hope Melanie didn't have anything to do with this. I don't think she would…"

"I'm sorry, Helen. But we have to investigate all the suspects," I said.

"I understand," Helen said.

"We'll let you know when we crack the case," Ashley said.

"I'll be ready for you to make another

batch of your ice cream as soon as you do," Helen promised.

I followed Ashley back into the kitchen. I watched as she added Charlie and Melanie to our list of suspects. It made me happy that Tim's name wasn't the only one on the list anymore.

"Let's do one more sweep for clues before we leave," Ashley suggested.

We divided the kitchen in half and searched all the cooking stations. I didn't find anything. Not a button or a piece of cloth or anything. "Nothing over here," I told Ashley.

"Nothing here either," she said. We grabbed our backpacks and headed out to our bikes.

"So we have three suspects. Three people who touched the cherry sauce," Ashley said. She knelt down to unlock her bike from the bike rack.

"But everybody was gone when we came out of the freezer," I said as I unlocked my bike. "Except Samantha—and she's not a suspect. So when did the thief have a chance to steal our ice cream?"

"That's an easy one," Ashley said. She dumped her lock and chain into her bike basket. "Everyone was probably busy getting ready to leave while we were in the freezer. The thief could have done everything right out in the open without anyone noticing."

I climbed on my bike. "Maybe we should think about motives," I said. *Motive* is a word we learned from our great-grandma Olive. She's a detective too. Motive is the reason a criminal has for committing a crime.

Ashley got on her bike. We began to pedal home. We pedaled slowly so we could talk.

"I can think of a motive for Tim," Ashley said. She didn't sound happy about it. "You know how much he loves ice cream. That means he really, really wants to win all those sundaes."

"And he *did* say our flavor was the best he ever tasted," I added. "He might have been afraid we would win the sundaes instead of him."

We stopped at a stop sign. "Melanie has a great motive too. She always has to have the best. And everyone agreed our ice cream was the best!" I said.

Ashley and I began to pedal again. "She would go nuts if her flavor didn't win," Ashley said. "Then it wouldn't be the best. You're right, Mary-Kate. She has a big reason for wanting our flavor out of the contest. She knows a lot of people would vote for it."

"How about Charlie?" I asked.

"Hmmm…I can't think of a good motive for Charlie," Ashley said. "He just wanted to have fun throwing in tons of different ingredients."

"And scrambling words," I added. We both laughed.

"You know what, Ashley? Right now I think Melanie is our number one suspect," I said.

"I think so too," Ashley said. "But we need more evidence. And fast!"

She slowed down and stood up on her pedals. "And we're on our way to getting some. I see a big clue right in front of us!"

6

YIKES, TIM!

"**D**o I need to get out my magnifying glass?" I asked. "Because I don't see a clue."

Ashley laughed. "It's really big. That's probably why you don't see it," she told me.

We had stopped at the bushes where we had found our ice cream container.

I studied the bushes. No clue. I stared down at the sidewalk. No clue. I looked up—and saw the clue! It was a sign that read BUS STOP.

"I bet our thief takes this bus! I bet he or she dumped our ice cream and then got on the bus!" I cried.

"It's definitely something we have to investigate," Ashley said. She grabbed a bus map from a plastic holder attached to the bus stop sign. "Let's ride fast. We have work to do!"

We made it home in record time and raced straight up to our detective office in the attic. Our basset hound, Clue, wagged her tail hello, then went straight back to sleep. She's the silent partner in the Olsen and Olsen Detective Agency.

Ashley spread the bus map out on our big desk. "Okay, we know where Tim lives. He's right near the corner of Hillary Drive and Margot Place."

I found Hillary Drive on the map and put my finger on it. Ashley put her finger on Margot Place. We moved our fingers toward each other. They met each other right by Tim's house.

I looked from that spot to the red line that showed the bus route. "Yikes," I said. "The bus goes right by Tim's house. That means he's an extra-good suspect."

Ashley picked up the phone book. "Let's see where Melanie lives. First we need to find her address." She flipped the pages until she got to the *S*'s. "Sweeney, Sweeney, Sweeney," she muttered.

I peered over her shoulder.

"There's Helen's telephone number," Ashley said. "And here's a Jack Sweeney."

"I bet Jack Sweeney is Melanie's dad." I grabbed the phone and dialed the number. A lady answered. "Hello, may I speak to Melanie, please?"

"She's not home right now. Can I take a message?" the lady asked.

"This is Mary-Kate Olsen," I said. "I'll call

back later. Thanks." I hung up. "That's the right Sweeney," I told Ashley.

"So we're looking for 3612 Stockton Avenue." Ashley scanned the map. "Here's Stockton. Oooh, and look! The bus runs down a street one block over."

"That means Melanie is still a good suspect. But we need to check out where Charlie lives." I turned to the *E* pages of the phone book. "Look—there are three Elliots listed."

Ashley grabbed the phone and dialed. There was no one named Charlie at the first number. Or the second. Or the third. "That's weird," Ashley said.

"Maybe his family isn't listed in the phone book. Not everyone is," I reminded her.

Ashley picked up her detective notebook. She wrote down our new clues. Tim and Melanie could have been at the bus stop where we found our melted ice cream. They both could have taken the bus home.

"Put a question mark under Charlie's address," I suggested.

Ashley did. Then she closed her notebook. "We can't do any more detecting tonight," she said.

"You're right," I said. "But we'll start snooping first thing in the morning. And you know where we have to snoop first."

"Yes, I do." Ashley grinned. "And I can't wait!"

Ashley studied our list. "The next candy store on our list is over by Sweet Sundaes," she said.

We pedaled to Chessa's Candies and parked our bikes in front. "I hope this is the store that sells the polka-dot jelly beans," I said.

"Me too. Because the jelly beans could

be the clue that leads us to our thief," Ashley said.

A bell over the door jangled as we stepped inside the candy store. I took a deep breath. I loved the way the store smelled. The air was a mix of cotton candy, chocolate, licorice, and a dozen other yummy things.

"The jelly beans are over there." Ashley pointed to a stack of plastic bins in the back of the store. We rushed over to them.

I spotted pink punch-flavored jelly beans. Brown coffee-flavored jelly beans. Green sour-apple jelly beans. And polka-dot jelly beans!

Ashley and I slapped a high five. We had tracked down the polka-dot jelly beans. That meant we were one step closer to tracking down our thief.

The bell on the candy store door jingled.

I looked over my shoulder. "Yikes!"

"Hey, Mary-Kate. Hey, Ashley," Tim called.

He hurried over to us. "I see you've found my favorite candy store ever!"

"Yikes," Ashley whispered.

7

CASE CLOSED?

"**L**et me give you a tour," Tim said. "Over there you got your pretzels. You can get them covered with marshmallows, with sprinkles, with caramel, with chocolate. The owner, Mr. Monroe, will cover them with anything you want. Once I had him dip one in milk chocolate and then roll it in red hots."

Tim closed his eyes and rubbed his stomach. "That was a great day," he said. "Now, right across from us is the candy jewelry. You guys might like that. There are candy necklaces and candy rings. There are even some candy fingernails you can eat right off your hands."

"Cool," Ashley said.

"There's one thing you absolutely have to try," Tim continued. "The polka-dot jelly beans. They're awesome."

"And how many of my awesome jelly beans do you want today, Tim?" a tall man with a gray mustache called from behind the cash register.

"Hi, Mr. Monroe!" Tim called back. "These are my friends Mary-Kate and Ashley. I'm telling them all about your store."

Mr. Monroe came out from behind the register. He used a silver scoop to fill a plastic bag with the polka-dot jelly beans. Then he handed the bag to Tim. "Today your favorites are on me. For being one of my favorite customers."

"Those are your favorites?" I asked.

"Absolute number one favorite," Tim answered.

Ashley pulled out her detective notebook and began to write.

"Mr. Monroe, do a lot of other kids buy those polka-dot jelly beans?" Ashley asked.

"There's a girl about your age who buys them every time she's in here," Mr. Monroe answered. "You should see her. She studies each jelly bean before she lets me put it in her sack. She says she buys only the best of the best."

That sounded like somebody we knew. Somebody who was also on our list of suspects! I put my hands behind my back and crossed my fingers. I crossed my toes too. "Does the girl have short curly red hair?" I asked.

"How did you know?" Mr. Monroe exclaimed.

"They are detectives. They know all kinds of stuff," Tim answered.

The bell on the door jangled. A woman with a big white poodle walked in. "Excuse me." Mr. Monroe hurried over to the other customer.

Ashley made a new entry in her detective notebook. Tim watched her. "Are you guys on a case right now?" he asked.

"Well…um…yes," I said.

"Who are you solving a crime for this time?" Tim said.

"Ourselves," Ashley answered. "Somebody stole the ice cream we made yesterday. We think it's somebody who is in the ice cream contest. They stole our recipe too. Now we have to find out who the thief is."

Tim's mouth dropped open. "You mean there won't ever be another batch of Creamy Orange Choco Chunk?" he cried.

"Don't worry about that," I answered.

"We're on the trail of the thief right now. The thief also stole our secret ingredient. And he or she left polka-dot jelly beans in its place."

"We know where the jelly beans are sold. That brings us a lot closer to the thief," Ashley explained.

"Hey, I buy the polka-dot jelly beans. And I'm in the ice cream contest." Tim laughed. "So am I your number one suspect?"

"Um," I said. "Well…"

Tim stopped laughing. "You mean I *am* your number one suspect?"

"Don't get upset, Tim," I said. "We don't really think you did it. But we have to follow all our clues. That is what detectives—"

"You think I'm a thief?" Tim interrupted me. "But I'm one of your best friends!"

"We don't think you did it," Ashley said again. "But we do have to study the evidence."

"Hey, kids." Mr. Monroe strolled back over to us, holding a bag of deep-red candies. "You have to try these. I just got them in. They are the sourest sour-cherry balls you've ever tasted. Your mouths won't unpucker for a week!"

Tim backed away from Mr. Monroe. "No thanks."

I stared at Tim. "You just turned down candy!" I burst out. "Are you feeling okay?"

Mr. Monroe reached out and put his hand on Tim's forehead. "He doesn't have a fever. But he must be sick!"

"I hate cherries," Tim explained. "I never eat them. Ever."

"But you were eating cherry sauce straight out of the jar at Sweet Sundaes," Ashley said.

"Nope. That was raspberry sauce," Tim said.

I grabbed his hand and shook it hard.

"Congratulations! You are now off our list of suspects!"

Ashley shook his hand too. "The thief left smears of cherry sauce on everything he or she touched. That means you're not the thief."

"I could have told you that!" Tim said. "So what are you going to do now?"

"We need more clues," I said.

"Let's head back to Sweet Sundaes," Ashley said. "Maybe we missed something."

"I'll come with you," Tim volunteered. "My stomach is asking for some ice cream."

"He's back to normal!" Ashley laughed.

"Thanks for the jelly beans, Mr. Monroe," Tim said.

We trooped out of the candy store. Then we hopped on our bikes and pedaled over to the ice cream shop.

Tim pointed through the front window. "Look! Charlie and Melanie are there."

"Great!" I said. The two suspects we had left were in one place. That was the perfect setup for clue hunting.

"Hey, guys—what are you doing?" Ashley called.

"I'm helping out my aunt with the big grand opening," Melanie answered.

"I'm doing a survey," Charlie said. "I'm keeping score of what kind of ice cream people buy."

"Why?" I asked.

"I thought maybe I could figure out who will win the contest tomorrow," Charlie explained. "So far, most people like chocolate. So I think a flavor that has some chocolate in it will have a better chance of winning. Hmmm…chocolate. What words can I make from those letters? 'Coca,' 'cola,' 'cool,' 'taco…'"

"I don't think your system will work," Melanie told Charlie. "I think people vote for the best. And I'm sure *mine* is the best!"

"Sounds like you're pretty sure you're going to win," Ashley said.

Melanie shrugged. "The best ingredients make the best ice cream. The best ice cream wins the contest. That's just how it is."

"But what if—" Tim began.

"Hey!" Melanie cried. She rushed over to a girl who had just come into the store. The girl was wearing a baseball cap that had WORLD'S *Best* BEST FRIEND printed on it.

"She didn't wait to hear my question," Tim complained.

"I want to trade you for that hat," Melanie told the girl. She was talking loud enough for everyone in the ice cream shop to hear her.

"Sorry," the girl with the cap said. "My best friend gave it to me."

Melanie pulled two sparkly barrettes out of her hair. "I'll give you these," she offered.

"They would look great on the ends of your braids."

"No thanks," the girl answered.

"Wait right there!" Melanie ordered.

She rushed back to us. She grabbed her backpack and started rooting through it. "I'll give you the barrettes and a butterfly pin," she called over her shoulder.

"I'm not trading the hat," the girl said.

"Wait!" Melanie began digging again. "I'll throw in some polka-dot jelly beans! They're fabulous."

Ashley pulled out her detective notebook.

"I really don't want to—" the girl began.

"Wait!" Melanie cried. "I'll give you some gummy oranges too. They're the world's best. The best! The very best!"

Whoa! Were those *our* World's Best Gummy Oranges?

"Ashley," I whispered. "I think we just found our thief!"

8

A NEW CLUE!

"**M**elanie, I think you have our secret Creamy Orange Choco Chunk ingredient!" Ashley said.

I jumped in. "Did you steal it from us?"

"I did not steal your secret ingredient!" Melanie shot back. She put her hands on her hips.

"But it's right there in your hands," I said.

"The gummy oranges are your secret ingredient?" Melanie's brown eyes opened wide as she looked from me to Ashley. "I didn't know that."

"Then why did you steal them?" Ashley asked.

"I didn't steal them. Stop saying that," Melanie said. "I traded you for them. Didn't you find the polka-dot jelly beans I left you?"

"It's not trading if you don't ask," Tim said.

"I just wanted the gummy oranges because it said they were the world's best on the package," Melanie explained. "You were in the freezer. That's why I didn't ask you. I didn't think you'd care."

"You should ask before you trade," I said.

"Next time I will," Melanie promised.

"Okay," Ashley said. "We have to ask Helen a question. Do you know where she is?"

"She's in her office," Melanie said.

"Bye, Tim. Bye, Melanie. Bye, Charlie," I called as we walked toward Helen's office.

Ashley grabbed my arm before I could knock on the door. "What do you think?" she asked. "Do you think Melanie stole our ice cream?"

"I don't know," I answered. "We thought the same person who stole our ice cream and recipe stole the secret ingredient. But we don't have proof."

I sighed. "So Melanie stays on our list of suspects."

Ashley nodded. She reached out and knocked on Helen's door.

"Come in," Helen called. "Have you two found your recipe?" she asked when we stepped inside.

"Not yet," I answered.

"We were wondering if we could check for more clues in the kitchen," Ashley said.

"Absolutely," Helen told us. "I'll be here if you need any help."

Ashley and I ran to the kitchen. Time

was running out. We had to find our recipe and make a new batch of Creamy Orange Choco Chunk before the store opened tomorrow. We had a new bag of gummy oranges. Great-grandma Olive had sent them to us.

"Uh-oh. It's going to be hard to find any new clues in here," Ashley said. "Helen cleaned up too well!"

I studied the kitchen. Every counter gleamed. The metal of the freezer door sparkled. The kitchen was so spotless I could eat ice cream off the floor!

"This is bad," I said. "We don't have any more clues. And a detective with no clues has nothing to detect with!"

Ashley stared at a row of ice cream containers lined up on one of the counters. "The green container!" Ashley shouted. "That's a clue!"

"You're right." I punched my fist into the

air. "Helen said that she didn't have any pale green containers. She said she would have known something was wrong if she had seen a green container."

Ashley snapped her fingers. "So the thief must have had the pale green container with him or her."

"Let's ask Helen where she buys her ice cream containers. Maybe we can track our thief that way!" I exclaimed.

"Here it is. The Cardboard Company," Ashley called.

We parked our bikes and hurried inside. A lady in a flowered dress sat behind a desk in the lobby. "I'm Ms. Andretti. How can I help you today?" she asked.

"We heard that you sell ice cream containers here," Ashley said. "Is that right?"

"We're the only place in town that does," Ms. Andretti answered.

I gave her my best smile. "We were wondering if you could tell us who buys pale green ice cream containers from you."

"Not a problem with my new computer!" Ms. Andretti patted the top of her monitor. Then she clicked some keys. "Okay, we sell the most pale green containers to O'Telli's Old-Fashioned Ice Cream Shoppe."

Ashley wrote that down in her detective notebook.

Ms. Andretti clicked some more keys. "Ms. Berg buys some pale green containers too."

"Ms. Berg? She was our second grade teacher," Ashley said. "She was great."

"I think she gives the containers to her students to store their art supplies in," Ms. Andretti said. "Let's see. Mrs. Sweeney also buys pale green containers. She likes to store sugar in them because they match her pale green kitchen."

"Mrs. Sweeney?" I could almost feel my ears perking up.

"Do you know if she has a daughter?" Ashley asked.

"Melanie. A little redhead," Ms. Andretti answered.

And we were off again. We pedaled as hard as we could over to Melanie's house.

Ashley and I were both out of breath when we knocked on her door. Melanie was home from the ice cream store. She answered the door holding a bowl…

…and the bowl was filled with Creamy Orange Choco Chunk!

9

MELANIE IS THE THIEF!

"**Y**ou said you didn't steal our recipe," I said before Melanie could open her mouth.

"I didn't," Melanie insisted.

"But you have Creamy Orange Choco Chunk right there in your bowl!" Ashley exclaimed.

"I bought this ice cream at O'Telli's," Melanie said. "I went there and bought a little bit of every flavor they had. I wanted to be sure my Best of the Best ice cream is the best ice cream ever. Not just the best ice cream at Sweet Sundaes."

Ashley and I stared at each other. I knew we were both wondering the same thing—was Melanie telling the truth?

Melanie shook her head. "You don't believe me? Come on, I'll show you." She led the way to her kitchen and opened the fridge. In the freezer were seven pale green cartons.

"Look." Melanie opened one of the cartons. "This is Cookie Surprise. Mine is better." She opened another carton. "This is Peanut Butter Dream. Mine is better." She started to open another carton.

"It's okay. You can stop," Ashley told her. "Where did you say you bought this ice cream?"

"At O'Telli's Old-Fashioned Ice Cream Shoppe over by the pet store," Melanie answered. "*Now* are you going to stop bugging me? I have lots more ice cream to taste."

"See you tomorrow night," I told her.

"When my flavor wins," Melanie said.

Ashley and I headed back to our bikes. "Do you believe her?" I asked Ashley.

"I don't know," Ashley said. "But Ms. Andretti said that O'Telli's buys the most light green containers. We should check it out."

"Right," I said. We got back on our bikes. And we pedaled and pedaled.

"There it is!" Ashley took one hand off her handlebars and pointed to a sign with pale green letters. It read O'TELLI'S.

A bus passed us. It stopped right in front of O'Telli's.

"Hey, that's the bus that runs by Sweet Sundaes," Ashley said.

"You're right! We should add that to the detective notebook," I said.

We parked our bikes and rushed inside.

Ashley skidded to a stop on the pale green floor and grabbed my arm.

"What's wrong, Ashley?" I asked.

She was staring at the chalkboard hanging over the ice cream counter. "I know who the thief is!"

10

AND THE WINNER IS...

I looked at the chalkboard too. The words "O'Telli and Son's Old-Fashioned Ice Cream Shoppe" were printed on it.

Then it hit me.

I looked at Ashley. "I know who it is too! Let's go."

Ashley and I marched up to the man behind the counter. He ran his hands down his green-and-white striped jacket. "Hello there. I'm Leo O'Telli, owner of the shop.

What can I get for you two lovely young ladies?"

"We'd each like a cone with the special orangy-chocolatey flavor," Ashley said.

"Excellent choice," Mr. O'Telli said. He picked up an ice cream scoop and got to work on the cones.

Mr. O'Telli handed Ashley and me each a cone. She took a lick. I took a bite.

"It's exactly like ours," Ashley whispered.

"Except without the gummy oranges," I whispered back.

That meant our recipe was in the ice cream shop right then. And maybe the thief was too!

"What do you think?" Mr. O'Telli gave us a big smile.

"It's great," I answered. "Who invented this flavor?"

"My son," Mr. O'Telli answered. "I'm thinking of changing the name of the place to O'Telli and Son's Old-Fashioned Ice Cream Shoppe!" He pointed to the chalk-board.

"How did your son come up with it?" Ashley asked.

"You can ask him yourself," Mr. O'Telli said. "Son, come on out here! There are some people who want to tell you how great your ice cream flavor is."

A pair of swinging doors to the left of Mr. O'Telli opened. And Charlie Elliot burst through. He had a big smile on his face.

The smile disappeared when he saw me and Ashley.

"These girls were asking all about your recipe," Mr. O'Telli told Charlie.

Charlie opened his mouth. Then shut it. It looked like he didn't know what to say.

"Hi, Charlie," I said. "Did you know that if you scramble the letters in the name Elliot you come up with the name O'Telli?"

Charlie gulped. He turned red and looked at the floor. "I guess you caught me," he said.

"Caught you doing what?" Mr. O'Telli asked.

"Um…well…I….I stole the recipe from them, Dad," Charlie mumbled.

"What?" Mr. O'Telli said. His smile was gone now too.

"I signed up for the contest at Sweet Sundaes. The one where you make your own flavor," Charlie continued.

He kept his gaze on his sneakers. "I wanted to be sure no one came up with a flavor that was better than any of ours."

"Go on," Mr. O'Telli said.

"Mary-Kate and Ashley came up with a fantastic flavor. I'd never tasted one so good," Charlie rushed on. "I was afraid that when Sweet Sundaes started selling it, all our customers would go over there."

"You had a green ice cream container with you, right?" Ashley asked Charlie.

"Right. I was bringing containers home to my dad," Charlie answered. "I'm sorry I stole your recipe." He looked back and forth from me to Ashley. "I was just worried about my dad's business."

"There's nothing to worry about," Mr. O'Telli said as he walked back up to us. "Business is good. And you know why?"

"Because everyone loves ice cream," Charlie answered. It sounded like something he'd said a hundred times before.

"Right!" Mr. O'Telli clapped Charlie on the shoulder. "And there are all kinds of people in the world. That means there needs to be all kinds of flavors. And all kinds of ice cream shops."

He winked at me and Ashley. "I'm planning to pay a visit to Sweet Sundaes myself. I love tasting new flavors."

Mr. O'Telli turned to Charlie. "And you will also be paying a visit to Sweet Sundaes. I expect you to tell Helen Sweeney what you did and apologize to her."

"'Seed,' 'load,' 'lose,' 'deal,' 'seal,' 'cad,'" Charlie began to mutter.

"What's he scrambling now?" Ashley asked me.

I grinned. "Those are the words you can make out of the letters in 'case closed'!"

Charlie gave us back our recipe and we made up a new batch of Creamy Orange Choco Chunk. Was it good enough to win the contest?

Late Sunday afternoon, everyone who entered the contest gathered at Sweet Sundaes. Even Charlie was there. Helen had accepted his apology.

Helen smiled at us. "Ready to hear who won?" she asked.

"Yes!" we all cheered.

"In third place is Samantha's flavor—Mom's French Toast!" Helen announced.

"Yay!" I yelled.

"Go, Samantha," Ashley cried.

"I knew mine wouldn't be third," Melanie said. "The best is always number one."

"In second place is Melanie's Best of the Best flavor," Helen continued.

"No way!" Melanie hollered over the clapping. "It can't be number two."

"But it is," Helen told her. "I counted the votes myself."

Then Helen cleared her throat. "And the number one flavor is…"

I squeezed Ashley's hand.

"It's a tie!" Helen said. "Mary-Kate and Ashley's Creamy Orange Choco Chunk and Tim's Monkey Chow!"

"Hooray!" Ashley and I shouted. We gave each other a high five.

Tim jumped up and down. "Free ice cream for a whole year!" he yelled. "This is the best day of my whole life!"

Charlie grinned at us. "Congratulations, Mary-Kate and Ashley! I'm glad you won."

"Thanks, Charlie," I said.

Charlie turned to Tim. "Tim's Monkey Chow? Hmmm..." He scrambled the letters in his head. "Who won? Honest Tim!"

Hi from both of us,

Ashley and I were so excited when we won the Paradise Pets raffle. We got lots of free pet supplies for our dog, Clue. And best of all, Clue won a chance to star in the opening show of the Barnaby Family circus! We couldn't wait!

But when we got to the circus, everything started to go wrong. It looked as if someone was trying to stop Clue from performing in the show!

Want to find out what happened? Turn the page for a sneak peek at *The New Adventures of Mary-Kate & Ashley: The Case of Clue's Circus Caper.*

See you next time!

Mary-Kate Olsen   *Ashley Olsen*

The Case Of
CLUE'S CIRCUS CAPER

"Introducing Penny Doodle and her Oodles of Poodles!" announced Benjamin Barnaby, the circus ringmaster.

A woman dressed in a glittery leotard and tights ran out from behind the curtain. Three little poodles ran right behind her on their hind legs!

My sister Ashley and I giggled. The poodles looked so cute in their pink tutus and rhinestone collars!

"Here are the winners of the Paradise Pets raffle," Benjamin said to Penny. "This is Mary-Kate and Ashley Olsen and their dog, Clue."

Penny's eyes widened as she stared at Clue. "You didn't tell me Clue was a basset hound," she said.

"What's wrong with basset hounds?" I asked.

"Basset hounds are too long to jump through hoops," Penny cried. "Their stomachs hang too low to wear tutus. And their long ears drag in the sawdust!"

"Does that mean Clue can't perform in the show?" Ashley asked in a worried voice.

"There must be *something* Clue can do," Ben said. He tugged at his black mustache as he thought. Then he snapped his fingers. "I got it! Why don't we make Clue a canine clown?"

"A clown?" I asked.

"Oh, yes, yes, yes!" Ben said excitedly. "We can dress Clue up in a funny pointy hat and ruffled collar. Then Penny can teach Clue some simple stunts. We can call the act—Oodles of Poodles...with a Hint of Hound!"

"Cool!" Ashley cheered.

"Hear that, girl?" I asked Clue. "You'll be exchanging your detective nose for a funny red rubber one!"

"In your dreams!" a gruff voice called out.

Ashley and I spun around. A clown wearing white makeup, a rubber nose, and a fuzzy green wig marched over. His giant shoes made thumping noises in the sawdust.

"Girls," Ben said. "I'd like you to meet Flip the Clown."

"You know I'm supposed to be the only clown in this circus!" Flip cried. "It's in my contract!" He yanked a scroll of paper from inside his jacket. It unrolled all the way down to the floor.

"See?" Flip demanded. "It's in the Chuckle Clause!"

"I do see," Ben said. "But the Chuckle Clause says nothing about canine clowns."

Flip's bald head turned red. "We'll just see about that!" he said. He stuffed his contract back into his jacket and stomped away.

"And I thought clowns were supposed to be funny," Ashley whispered to me.

"Me too," I said. "Do you think—"

"Look out!" Penny yelled.

I looked up and gasped. A caramel-colored horse was galloping across the ring straight at us!

THE NEW ADVENTURES OF MARY-KATE & ASHLEY
Movie Madness Party Sweepstakes

OFFICIAL RULES:

1. No purchase necessary.

2. To enter complete the official entry form or hand print your name, address, age, and phone number along with the w "THE NEW ADVENTURES OF MARY-KATE & ASHLEY Movie Madness Party Sweepstakes" on a 3" x 5" card and mail to: THE ADVENTURES OF MARY-KATE & ASHLEY Movie Madness Party Sweepstakes, c/o HarperEntertainment, Attn: Children's Mark Department, 10 East 53rd Street, New York, NY 10022. Entries must be received **no later than April 30, 20** Enter as often as you wish, but each entry must be mailed separately. One entry per envelope. Partially completed, ille or mechanically reproduced entries will not be accepted. Sponsors are not responsible for lost, late, mutilated, illegible, stolen, po due, incomplete, or misdirected entries. All entries become the property of Dualstar Entertainment Group, LLC., and will not be retu

3. Sweepstakes open to all legal residents of the United States (excluding Colorado and Rhode Island), who are between the ag five and fifteen by April 30, 2003, excluding employees and immediate family members of HarperCollins Publishers, ("HarperCollins"), Parachute Properties and Parachute Press, Inc., and their respective subsidiaries and affiliates, officers, dire shareholders, employees, agents, attorneys, and other representatives (individually and collectively "Parachute"), Du Entertainment Group, LLC., and its subsidiaries and affiliates, officers, directors, shareholders, employees, agents, attorneys other representatives (individually and collectively "Dualstar"), and their respective parent companies, affiliates, subsidi advertising, promotion and fulfillment agencies, and the persons with whom each of the above are domiciled. Offer void w prohibited or restricted by law.

4. Odds of winning depend on the total number of entries received. Approximately 250,000 sweepstakes announcements publi All prizes will be awarded. Winners will be randomly drawn on or about May 15, 2003, by HarperCollins, whose decisions are Potential winner will be notified by mail and will be required to sign and return an affidavit of eligibility and release of liability in 14 days of notification. Prizes won by minors will be awarded to parent or legal guardian who must sign and return all rec legal documents. By acceptance of the prize, winner consents to the use of his or her name, photograph, likeness, and per information by HarperCollins, Parachute, Dualstar, and for publicity purposes without further compensation except where prohi

5. One (1) **Grand Prize Winner** wins a Movie Madness Party for the winner and 10 friends which consists of the follo nine (9) videos starring Mary-Kate and Ashley (WHEN IN ROME, GETTING THERE, HOLIDAY IN THE SUN, WINNING LONDON, SC DANCE PARTY, OUR LIPS ARE SEALED, PASSPORT TO PARIS, BILLBOARD DAD, and SWITCHING GOALS; $250.00 worth of movie es to a movie theater chain to be chosen by sponsor; food (including popcorn, soda, six foot deli sub sandwich, deli sal Approximate retail value: $585.00.

6. Only one prize will be awarded per individual, family, or household. Prizes are non-transferable and cannot be sold or redeem cash. No cash substitute is available. Any federal, state, or local taxes are the responsibility of the winner. Sponsor may subs prize of equal or greater retail value, if necessary, due to availability.

7. Additional terms: By participating, entrants agree a) to the official rules and decisions of the judges, which will be final respects; and to waive any claim to ambiguity of the official rules and b) to release, discharge, and hold harmless HarperC Parachute, Dualstar, and their affiliates, subsidiaries, and advertising and promotion agencies from and against any and all lic or damages associated with acceptance, use, or misuse of any prize received in this Sweepstakes.

8. Any dispute arising from this Sweepstakes will be determined according to the laws of the State of New York, without referer its conflict of law principles, and the entrants consent to the personal jurisdiction of the State and Federal courts located in York County and agree that such courts have exclusive jurisdiction over all such disputes.

9. To obtain the name of the winners, please send your request and a self-addressed stamped envelope (residents of Vermont omit return postage) to Movie Madness Party Sweepstakes Winners, c/o HarperEntertainment, Attn: Children's Mark Department, 10 East 53rd Street, New York, NY 10022 by June 1, 2003. Sweepstakes Sponsor: HarperCollins Publishers,

The Ultimate Fa...

mary-kat

Don't miss

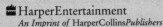

HarperEntertainment
An Imprint of HarperCollins*Publishers*

PARACHUTE PRESS

DUALSTAR PUBLICATIONS

mary-kateandashley
America Online Keyword: mary-kate

Mary-Kate as Misty

Ashley as Amber

t's go
e the world...
gain!

MARY-KATE AND ASHLEY in ACTION!

only on

TOON Disney CHANNEL

DUALSTAR ANIMATION

Dualstar Entertainment Group, LLC

Call your cable operator or satellite provider to request Toon Disney.

ToonDisney.com ©Disney

Six **HOT** collections of music you LOVE from the **mary-kateandashley** brand

It's What YOU Listen To

THE HIT TELEVISION SERIES –
OW AVAILABLE ON VIDEO AND DVD!

It's What YOU Watch.

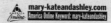

Distributed by